Book 1

THE SECRET DOOR

Written by Jenny Phillips

Illustrations by Kessler Garrity
Cover Illustration by Brandon Dorman

Mrs. Bastian's House

Books in the Badger Hills Farm Series

TABLE OF CONTENTS

CHAPTER 1

TIMOTHY STIRRED AND SAT UP IN BED, rubbing his eyes. A soft "coo-oo" followed by three louder "coos" floated through the air.

What is that sound, and where is it coming from? he thought. It was his first morning waking up in his new home at Badger Hills Farm.

"Coo-oo, coo, coo, coo" came the soft call again, this time followed by the thud of running feet as Timothy's cousin, Zoey, came dashing down the hallway.

Zoey and her grandmother, Nanna Bell, had come to live with Timothy and his father, John, shortly after Zoey's mom had passed away. Timothy had lost his mother, too, but long ago, when he was a baby. The children had

grown to be more like siblings to each other than cousins.

Zoey burst into the room, excitement written all over her face. Zoey's big ideas and bright personality had surprised Timothy at first, but now he loved her spirited ways.

With her curly hair flying, Zoey dashed to Timothy's large window. "It's a mourning dove!" she cried. "Come see! It has a nest in the pine tree right outside your window. Living at Badger Hills Farm is going to be amazing!"

She stopped suddenly and whirled around to Timothy.

"Oh no!" Zoey's eyes were wide. "I hope you were already getting up when I burst in. I was just so excited about that dove!"

Timothy chuckled. "It's all right, Zoey. I was already awake. But I do need to get dressed and say my prayers."

Zoey gave her cousin a quick hug and skipped out the door. Timothy crossed to the window, thanking God for the nest and all of His other beautiful creations. As he slipped a sweater over his T-shirt, the smell of Nanna Bell's delicious blueberry muffins tickled his nose. He bounded down the stairs toward the kitchen, with Zoey right on his heels.

"Good morning! You two slept in a little today," Nanna Bell said cheerfully as she flipped bacon that was sizzling and popping in her frying pan. "You must have been tired from the big move yesterday."

Timothy looked at some empty moving

boxes scattered on the kitchen counter. *What a whirlwind of a week!* he thought, reflecting on his father's marriage to Miss Lily two days before and the big move the day after their wedding.

Having come from a small city apartment, which was only a ten-minute walk from Badger Hills Farm, they hadn't had to move too many things. Most of their belongings had been put away yesterday before John and Lily left for their nine-day honeymoon.

As the cousins enjoyed Nanna Bell's delicious breakfast, Zoey gazed out the window. "Wow, that's a lot of fog rolling in. Look, Timothy."

"That is a lot of fog!" Timothy frowned. "I was hoping we could explore Badger Hills Farm

today, now that it's actually ours. I want to make a map of the grounds, but all that fog will make it hard. We might have to wait until tomorrow."

"A map is a great idea! We have 180 acres to explore!" Zoey exclaimed excitedly.

"Well, 177 to be exact," said Timothy with a smile. "Remember that Mrs. Bastian owns three acres."

"And can you believe you own the rest, Timothy?"

"Well, technically my dad owns it until I'm twenty-five, but no, I still can't believe it." Timothy picked up a piece of bacon and continued to gaze out the window. "I wonder how long it will take until this fog clears. It's covering almost everything outside."

"I'm sure it won't last all day," Zoey said as

she pulled out a notebook with a bright purple cover. "Hey, I wrote about how we got the farm. Do you want me to read it to you?"

"Sure," Timothy said with a smile. After meeting the famous author Bailey Bastian, who was their only neighbor on the farm, Zoey had decided she wanted to be a writer too.

She cleared her throat, held out her notebook, and began to read.

Two hundred years ago, a family with the last name of Roach purchased 180 acres of beautiful land, complete with a large pond, waving grass, rolling hills, several groves of thick woods, and a gurgling stream.

As the family began to work the land, they discovered a surprise on the farm—a den of badgers. Thus, they called their land "Badger Hills Farm."

The family decided never to sell the land. They handed it down from generation to generation.

Over time, a town grew up around Badger Hills Farm. The town turned into a small city and then into a large city.

Badger Hills Farm was surrounded by the city's streets and buildings.

The last generation of the Roach family had only one child, who outlived his relatives and had no children of his own to inherit the farm.

That is how Mr. Roach found himself the only surviving member of the Roach family. He was a very grumpy man with no friends . . . until an eleven-year-old boy named Timothy Todd came along.

"I'm twelve years old now," Timothy said after finishing his last sip of orange juice.

"Yes," replied Zoey, "but you were eleven when we met Mr. Roach last year. Keep listening." She began reading again.

Timothy and his family lived in a small city apartment close to Badger Hills Farm and loved to walk around the land, admiring its natural beauty.

Mr. Roach ran out of money, and the farm fell into disrepair. Eventually, he sold three acres to the famous author Bailey Bastian. This gave Mr. Roach enough money to live, but no one knew who would inherit the rest of Badger Hills Farm.

One day, Timothy's family was walking around the farm when they heard Mr. Roach calling for help, and that's how Timothy's family met Mr. Roach.

Timothy was kind to Mr. Roach and made him some paintings, for Timothy was an artist.

Sadly, Mr. Roach soon passed away. To everyone's great surprise, Mr. Roach left the farm to Timothy, to be in the care of Timothy's father until Timothy turned twenty-five.

I know this story well because I am Timothy Todd's cousin, and I just moved with him to Badger Hills Farm, where I am sure great adventures await.

"What a great story," Nanna Bell declared. "And now we're here, and you're right—who knows what adventures await us at Badger Hills Farm?"

Timothy's gaze drifted again to the window. A blanket of white shrouded all but a few pine boughs that poked their long arms from the dense fog. Nanna Bell's words echoed in Timothy's mind: *Who knows what adventures await us at Badger Hills Farm?*

CHAPTER 2

T HE GRAVEL ROAD CRUNCHED UNDER
their feet as Timothy and Zoey walked to
Mrs. Bastian's house. They had eaten breakfast,
finished their homeschool studies, and helped
unpack the remaining moving boxes. Nanna
Bell wanted them to visit Mrs. Bastian and let
her know they were all settled in.

A fluffy ball of light brown fur ran along
with them, pulling at his leash and sniffing
everything excitedly. It was Sammy, Timothy's

four-month-old puppy.

Badger Hills Farm seemed to be sleeping under its thick white blanket of fog. All was quiet until Sammy sighted a fuzzy gray squirrel scampering up a tree. He barked as fiercely as a puppy can. Timothy and Zoey giggled as the startled squirrel disappeared into the forest.

In Mrs. Bastian's library, Timothy told her that they were mostly unpacked already.

"When does your father get back from his honeymoon?" Mrs. Bastian asked, motioning Timothy, Zoey, and Sammy toward a plush sofa.

"In eight days," Timothy responded as he sat down. Sammy curled up in a soft brown ball at Timothy's feet, opening his mouth in a big puppy yawn. He was worn out from the walk and was soon fast asleep.

"Are you excited to have Lily as your stepmom?" Mrs. Bastian asked.

"Yes!" exclaimed Timothy. "Miss Lily is fun and kind, and she makes us so happy."

"That's right," Zoey agreed. "Since that first day meeting her in the library, we have just loved her!"

"So if my counting is correct, they will get back a few days before Christmas," Mrs. Bastian noted. "In the meantime, what are you two going to do?"

"We want to explore Badger Hills Farm!" Timothy cried. "We have lots of time to explore after our homeschool work is done each morning."

"Don't forget about our new chores," Zoey chimed in. "We didn't have many chores when we lived in our apartment, but we will need to do a lot of chores here, which I don't mind."

"Oh, that's right!" Timothy responded. "My dad left us a list of things to get started on. There's so much to do to fix up Badger Hills Farm."

"That's true." Mrs. Bastian nodded. "Mr. Roach tended his house and garden carefully, but he didn't do much to keep up the rest of the farm for the last fifty years of his life. Many of the trails are grown over, fences have rotted away, and the rock walls are crumbling. Zoey, you've already told me that you can't wait to fix up the horse-riding arena."

"That's right! And we need to build a barn so that we can bring Misty Toes and her foal over to our place. Thanks again so much for taking care of my horses for now."

Mrs. Bastian smiled at Miss Brown, her assistant, who walked in with a tray of steaming mugs.

"Ah, here's some wassail," Mrs. Bastian said. "I always enjoy serving it during the Christmas season."

Timothy took a sip. "Mmmm, tastes like apple cider, oranges, and cinnamon." The library's colorful holiday decorations and the warm, comforting drink felt especially like Christmas to Timothy.

The friends chatted about their plans for the farm as they sipped the wassail.

When Zoey had finished, she asked, "May we go to the barn to see Misty Toes and her foal?"

"Of course! You may go to the barn anytime you'd like," Mrs. Bastian replied.

Timothy stood up, too, tugging lightly on Sammy's leash. "I still can't believe you found Misty Toes and bought her back for Zoey. How did you find her?"

"Well, after hearing Zoey's story about having to sell her beloved horse and come live in the city, I had my assistant help me search until we found Misty Toes."

"And her new foal too!" cried Zoey. "I don't know how I can ever thank you!"

"It was my pleasure!" said Mrs. Bastian. "And they can stay in my barn as long as it takes for you to get your own barn. By the way, what are you going to name the little foal?"

"I'm not sure yet," replied Zoey. "I'll have to

give that some thought."

Timothy and Zoey thanked Mrs. Bastian
for the wassail and said their goodbyes before
heading to the door, little Sammy trotting
along behind.

"Oh, wait!" cried Mrs. Bastian. "I almost
forgot to ask you. Did you find a secret door at
your house?"

"A secret door?" asked Timothy. "No, we
don't know anything about a secret door. How
do you know about it?"

"Well," said Mrs. Bastian, "Mr. Roach
told me."

"What did he say?" asked Zoey excitedly.

"When he told me he was giving Badger
Hills Farm to your family, he said something
like 'I need to make sure Timothy knows about

the secret door in that house. I found the door later in my life.' But then he had a coughing fit and couldn't tell me any more. He passed away before I could ask him more about the door."

"Wow!" Timothy exclaimed. "I guess we have more exploring to do than we thought!"

CHAPTER 3

AFTER BRUSHING MISTY TOES AND playing with her foal for a while, Timothy and Zoey started back down the gravel road toward their house. Sammy followed along happily. Little bits of hay stuck out all over his fur—leftovers from his adventures exploring the barn. The fog still hadn't lifted, and the air felt wet and heavy.

"A secret door," Zoey half whispered. "How exciting! I wonder if there's a brick we'll push on to make a door swing open. Do you think we can find it today if we start searching?"

"Maybe. What in the world would a secret door lead to?" Timothy wondered aloud.

Just then, Sammy started barking. Before Timothy could stop him, he had sped off into the trees and disappeared into the fog.

"Sammy!" Timothy yelled, suddenly wishing he had put Sammy's leash back on before they left the barn.

"He probably heard a squirrel," Zoey said as she stopped, looking hard through the white-and-gray mist swirling around them.

"Sammy! Come on, Sammy!" called Timothy. The barking had stopped. "Man, I really need to teach Sammy to obey better."

"Yeah," agreed Zoey, "he's such a great dog, but he does need to learn to obey. I don't think we should follow him, though. It's too foggy."

"Sammy!" Timothy called again.

"Listen," said Zoey in a whisper. "I hear Sammy barking, but it sounds far away. Maybe the fog is just muting the sound."

"Rats!" Timothy said. "What should we do? I want to get back to the house and look for that door, but we can't leave Sammy. Come on. I bet he's not that far."

Timothy stepped off the gravel and walked toward the woods.

"I don't think we should go off the road in this fog," Zoey said again. "We don't know Badger Hills Farm that well, and we might get lost." She watched as the fog wrapped around Timothy.

He stopped. "I don't hear Sammy barking anymore. I wonder if something is wrong!"

Timothy started off into the trees again, faster this time.

"Wait!" Zoey called after him. She hesitated a moment before following.

The woods surrounded the cousins with startling beauty. The fog made everything feel mysterious. They hadn't gone far when the sound of gurgling water reached their ears.

"Look! The stream!" Timothy said, pointing to a sparkling ribbon of water flowing through the trees. "I love this stream! I could see it from the city street when we used to walk around Badger Hills Farm."

"It really is a fantastic stream," Zoey agreed, "just big enough to have a nice gurgling sound and to move happily along, but not so big that you can't jump over it in places."

"Listen, I hear Sammy barking again, and he sounds pretty close. We should keep going," Timothy said as he leaped over a narrow bend in the stream.

Zoey followed close behind. They soon came to a tall steel fence, behind which Sammy was running back and forth, barking.

"Sammy! How did you get on the other side?" Timothy cried. He turned to Zoey. "Let's see if we can find a gate or something so we can get him out and go home."

"This is the deer fence!" Zoey's eyes brightened with the realization. "Do you remember when Mr. Roach told us that thirty acres of the property are fenced in so that the deer don't go out into the city and get hurt?"

"That's right!" Timothy said as the two kids walked along the fence, looking for an opening.

Sammy followed along, his tail wagging, completely unaware of the trouble his mischief had caused.

They moved slowly through the thick fog. It was hard to see much farther than a few feet in front of them.

"This fog is getting thicker," Zoey observed.

"I agree," Timothy replied. "But we have to keep following the fence so we can get Sammy out. There was probably a hole underneath it somewhere that he squeezed through."

Zoey nodded. "You're probably right."

After following the fence for a few minutes, Zoey suddenly pointed and cried out, "It's a gate!"

They ran the short distance to the gate and noticed there was a small sign that read, "No Trespassing." Mr. Roach had put the sign up to keep people from letting the deer out. In no time, they had the gate open for Sammy. Just then, a flash of motion nearby caught Sammy's attention. He bounded away from the gate, barking, to chase after a group of deer.

"No! Come back, Sammy!" Timothy called as he and Zoey ran off after the little dog.

Suddenly, they were surrounded by a wall of white. The fog was so thick that they couldn't even see each other.

"Timothy!" Zoey called frantically.

"I'm here!" Timothy called back. "Don't move!"

His mind raced, wondering what they should do. Zoey sounded close, but he didn't want to move and risk being separated.

"I know!" he called out suddenly.

Zoey raised an eyebrow, turning toward the sound of his voice. "You know what?"

"Sing a song so I can follow the sound of your voice," he called back.

"Oh! That's a great idea!" Zoey started singing the first Christmas carol that popped into her head—"Away in a Manger." In just a few seconds, Timothy was giving her a big hug.

"Phew!" Zoey exclaimed, hugging him back tightly. "I've never been so happy to give you a hug!"

Timothy jumped as he simultaneously heard a bark and felt something bump his leg. It was Sammy!

"Sammy!" Timothy scolded, picking up his small dog and tucking him under his arm. "You're not going anywhere."

The two looked around, deciding which way to go. "Let's try to find the fence and follow it until we reach a gate," Zoey offered.

They started back in what they hoped was the right direction. It wasn't as easy to find the fence as they thought it would be. When Timothy finally spotted the wire grid of the fence through the fog, he breathed a sigh of relief. "Now all we have to do is follow this along until we find a gate."

Timothy felt sudden warmth from sunlight washing over his face. "The fog is lifting, Zoey!"

Once the fog decided to give way to the sunshine, it disappeared quickly. The children could now see the beautiful blue sky.

"I can tell by the sun that it's well past lunch," Zoey said.

"I can tell it's way past lunch just by how hungry I am!" joked Timothy.

After a few minutes, they finally came to a gate.

"This isn't the one we came through before." Zoey noticed that there was no sign on it. "I wonder how many gates there are along the fence?"

"We'll find out and mark them on our map," Timothy replied. "For now, I'm anxious to get back home to eat."

Zoey laughed. "And I'm anxious to find the secret door."

CHAPTER 4

Nanna Bell was as interested in the secret door as Zoey and Timothy were. "Hurry and finish eating so we can start looking around!" she said, a twinkle in her eye.

Timothy laughed and swallowed a mouthful of savory vegetable stew. "Nanna Bell is the best grandma ever, isn't she?"

Zoey smiled and nodded, finishing her last bite of warm buttered bread with a contented sigh.

"I'm sorry again that we worried you by being so late," Timothy said to Nanna Bell. "Thankfully, the fog lifted, so we could find our way home."

"You're both OK, and that's what matters," Nanna Bell replied. "When your father returns, I'll ask him if we can get each of you a phone watch. I'd feel more comfortable if you could call me if there's trouble when you're out and about."

"Great idea!" said Timothy, taking his empty bowl to the sink. "All right! Let the search begin. Let's find this secret door!"

Nanna Bell turned on Christmas music, and the group went from room to room, pushing on every part of each wall and looking for any type of button or lever.

They found nothing in the kitchen, but they hadn't really expected to find the secret door there. The library seemed the next logical place. After all, hidden passages in movies are often behind some library shelf. But they didn't find a secret door in the library either.

Next, they tried the guest room on the main floor. Then they searched the family room, but none of the bricks on the huge fireplace opened a secret door. Even though they checked every inch of Nanna Bell's, Zoey's, and Timothy's bedrooms, including the closets, they didn't find a secret door in any of them.

"I'm exhausted," said Zoey. "We've been at this for two hours."

"We only have the bathrooms and my father and Miss Lily's room left," Timothy said

encouragingly, even though he was tired too.

"Can we go into their room even though they're gone?" Zoey asked Nanna Bell.

"I don't think they will mind," Nanna Bell replied.

Half an hour later, the discouraged group flopped down in the chairs by the big fireplace in the family room.

"Nothing," Timothy moaned as he looked out the window. "And the sun is starting to set. We'll have to wait until tomorrow to start exploring and mapping the land."

Sammy rested his furry head on Timothy's lap and let out a little whine as if he could sense Timothy's disappointment.

Zoey sighed. "Maybe Mr. Roach was just imagining a secret door. People can sometimes forget things as they get older. Maybe there really isn't a door."

"I don't know," Nanna Bell said. "I think we searched everywhere, but let's not be too discouraged. How would you two like to do something special tonight?"

"What do you have in mind?" Timothy asked.

"Well, I thought I could show you both how to chop some wood. There are a few logs in the backyard, and I found the axe that your father bought last week."

Timothy raised his eyebrows, and Zoey laughed.

"That's your special idea?" Zoey asked.

"It's the start of my special idea." Nanna Bell smiled playfully.

"Sure!" Timothy said, standing up. "Let's

go before it starts getting too dark."

As the setting sun painted the pine trees with warm orange-and-pink light, the cousins learned how to chop wood safely.

"This is so much fun!" Zoey giggled as she picked up the pieces of wood she had just cut and put them in a pile. "I didn't know you could chop wood, Nanna Bell."

"Of course I can," replied Nanna Bell. "I haven't done it for many years, but I could never forget. It was one of my chores on our family farm when I was a teenager."

"You're right, Zoey. This is fun!" Timothy smiled, swinging the axe and watching the log break into two pieces as he struck it.

Before long, dusky shadows were falling over the backyard.

"That's enough firewood," Nanna Bell declared. "Let's put the axe away and go inside for the next part of our special night!"

Nanna Bell always knows how to have a good time, Timothy thought with a wide smile.

With their freshly cut wood, Nanna Bell started the first fire since they moved into the house. For safety's sake, she pushed a large screen in front of the fireplace. The metal mesh of the screen kept all the embers from popping out onto the floor.

"Wow," said Zoey, who was sitting in one of the big stuffed chairs by the crackling fire. "I love the smell of the wood."

"It's from a walnut tree, I believe," Nanna Bell said. "I just love the smell. It's one of my favorites. Now, does anyone know what holiday is coming up in two weeks?" she teased.

"Easter!" exclaimed Timothy, laughing so hard that he fell out of his chair.

Zoey shook her head at Timothy's silliness, but she couldn't help laughing at how hard Timothy was laughing. Sammy joined in the fun, jumping all over Timothy and licking his face.

"It's Christmas that's coming up, of course!" cried Zoey. "Are we going to do

something special to get in the Christmas spirit?"

"That's what I was thinking," Nanna Bell said as Timothy regained control of himself and sat back in his chair.

Nanna Bell stood up. "We don't have a Christmas tree this year since we had to throw our fake one away when we moved. It was too worn out and tattered to keep. But we can still make it feel like Christmas."

Nanna Bell then clapped her hands together with a big smile on her face. "Does anyone know what you can do with butter, white chocolate chips, popcorn, peppermint flavor, and crushed candy canes?"

"Eat them!" Timothy called.

"Yes," replied Nanna Bell, "but first we can

put all of those ingredients together to make peppermint popcorn balls."

"Wahoo!" sang Zoey. "That sounds so good!"

"And then, as you eat the popcorn balls," continued Nanna Bell, "I thought we could sit around the glowing fire, and I could start reading one of my favorite Christmas books to you. There are eleven chapters, so if we start tonight, and I read you a chapter every night, we can finish a few days before Christmas. What do you guys think?"

"I think that sounds wonderful," Timothy declared.

CHAPTER 5

THE GRAY ASHES WERE COOLING IN THE fireplace, and the house was dark and still.

It's too still, Timothy thought. He wasn't yet used to the quiet of the country setting. *And it's too dark*. The moonlight cast shadows of the swaying pine trees onto his walls. There were no bright city lights, humming cars, or blaring sirens here.

A loud "Whoo, whoo!" blared out in the quiet night.

Timothy nearly jumped out of his pajamas as he sat straight up in bed.

It's just an owl, he realized. He tried to calm his racing heart, but his room still felt too dark.

His bare feet padded quickly across the wooden floor to the bathroom connected to his room. Reaching in, Timothy flipped the light switch on and shut the door halfway. The golden slant of light across the floor was comforting. He snuggled down into his bed and closed his eyes. The soft swishing of the pine boughs in the gusty night air was no longer scary, though the light did make it more difficult to fall asleep.

Suddenly, Timothy sat bolt upright and let out a long, unhappy groan. *Rats!* he thought, remembering the first gate they had opened at the deer fence that day. *I was so worried about the fog and Sammy that I forgot to close the gate behind us when we went in. Then we went out a different gate. The deer might get out and go into the city!*

Timothy briefly considered snuggling back under the nice warm covers and forgetting the gate. But he knew he wouldn't sleep peacefully. His father had taught him to make the right choice, even when it was difficult. With a deep sigh, he got out of bed, put his boots on, and slipped a sweater over his pajama shirt.

The floorboards creaked under his weight as he made his way down the hall to wake up Zoey and Nanna Bell. By the time they were dressed, Timothy had turned on half the lights in the house to chase away the looming shadows. Deciding to leave Sammy at home was hard, but Timothy couldn't risk having the puppy run off again.

I was never scared of the dark before, thought Timothy as the group left the house, each with a large lantern.

"I like Badger Hills Farm a lot more in the daytime," he whispered as they started down the gravel road. The wind moaned through the tall dark trees.

Zoey moved closer to Nanna Bell. "Yes, even the crunching of the gravel sounds a lot happier in the daytime," she agreed.

"Where was it that you left the road to go find Sammy?" Nanna Bell asked. "Are we getting close?"

Zoey put her finger to her chin as she thought. "Hmmm . . . well, I do remember a big boulder I had to go around when we went off the path. I'll watch for it."

It wasn't long until Zoey spotted the boulder, and the group veered off the road.

"I'm not sure where the gate is from here," Timothy said. "It was so foggy, and now it's hard to see because it's dark. I do remember that we came to a stream and jumped over it, and then the fence wasn't much farther."

"Let's be quiet and listen for the stream," suggested Zoey.

Timothy shivered as they walked into the forest. The tall trees blocked out the moonlight, casting the forest floor into darkness. *Walking in this forest in the dark is much worse than walking on the wide gravel road*, he thought.

When the gurgling sound of the creek reached his ears, he breathed a sigh of relief. *At least something in this forest still sounds merry and bright at night.*

They quickly found the narrow bend in the stream and hopped to the other side. Soon their lantern beams sparkled on the wide-open metal gate.

"There it is!" cried Zoey, pointing.

Timothy held his lantern up higher. The light reflected off a pair of green eyes staring right at them. The group froze as the eyes came out through the open gate.

"I think it's a skunk," Zoey whispered. "I think I saw a stripe on it."

"It's not a skunk," Nanna Bell said quietly and calmly.

The dark form melted into the darkness beyond their lanterns.

"It's gone now," Nanna Bell whispered. "Let's hurry and shut the gate and get home." She put her hand on Timothy's shoulder. "I don't like being out here at night either, but it's OK. We're not in danger."

Timothy had never felt so scared. As soon as the gate was shut, he urged the group back over the stream and through the forest as quickly as he could, nearly stumbling several times on rocks and tree roots.

Timothy finally began to relax when he felt the familiar crunch of the gravel road beneath his feet. The windows of their home, glowing with golden light from within, soon came into view. Timothy was so thankful for that beautiful light.

As soon as they were inside, Nanna Bell hugged the children. "I'm so proud of you both. That was certainly an adventure."

"Not the kind of adventure I like," Timothy stated.

"I know, but you did the right thing, even though you knew it wouldn't be easy," Nanna Bell said with a smile. "Now, off to bed!"

As soon as he was in his room, Timothy stripped off his boots and sweater.

Darkness in my room is so much better than darkness outside, he thought. *But I still don't like the dark.*

Once more, he flipped the light on in his

bathroom and then shut the bathroom door halfway.

Before getting in bed, he knelt and thanked God for keeping them safe and for helping him do the right thing by choosing to go out and close the gate.

Then he gratefully slipped under his puffy quilt. He felt safe enough now to think about the creature with the shining green eyes. He remembered that Nanna Bell had said it wasn't a skunk. *What was it then? What has green eyes and a stripe? I need to remember to ask Nanna Bell in the morning.*

He closed his eyes as sleepiness washed over him.

CHAPTER 6

SUNLIGHT POURED THROUGH THE WINDOWS
the next morning, bathing the room
in pale yellow light. Timothy slipped on
a long-sleeved shirt to keep out the cool
December weather. Snow this time of year
would be unusual, but it did get cold enough
for long-sleeved shirts and sweaters and
sometimes even light jackets and coats.

Timothy hurriedly tied his shoes and raced
downstairs, where he found Zoey and Nanna

Bell setting breakfast out on the table.

"I just thought of something a little worrisome!" Timothy proclaimed.

"Wait! I'm starving. Let's pray over breakfast," Zoey said, "and then you can tell us all about it."

"Good idea," Timothy agreed as he took his place at the little table and breathed in the smell of steaming cinnamon oatmeal.

After they prayed, Timothy took a deep breath and revealed his worry. "Last night, we saw that creature with green eyes." Timothy tried not to shudder as he continued. "It was in the fenced area, but then we saw it come through the gate. Now it could be anywhere. Even in our backyard!"

Zoey pondered this information and then

added her own worries. "If it were a skunk, that wouldn't be too scary, but Nanna Bell, you said it wasn't a skunk. Do you know what it was?"

Nanna Bell smiled. "Yes, I do. I'll tell you—after you finish your breakfast."

Timothy took a bite of Nanna Bell's famous oatmeal and sighed. This was no ordinary oatmeal. Hot roasted pecans, cinnamon, and thick cream were swirled in.

"You know," Timothy remarked with a big grin, "before you and Zoey came to live with us, I ate cold cereal for breakfast every day, and we usually ate nachos or quesadillas for dinner. Our family's menu has greatly improved thanks to you, Nanna Bell. I'm so grateful for you, not just for your amazing cooking—for everything!"

"Well, I love to cook, and I love all of you, so it's my pleasure," Nanna Bell graciously replied.

All three ate silently for a while. The delicious, warm oatmeal was the perfect breakfast for the chilly winter morning. Zoey took the last bite and licked her spoon. "I wonder how Uncle John and Miss Lily are enjoying their trip?" she asked.

"Wait!" Timothy chimed in. "She's not Miss Lily anymore. She's Mrs. Lily, but I think it would be weird if we called her Mrs. Lily."

"Yeah," agreed Zoey, "and it feels weird to just call her Lily as well. What should we call her?"

"Hmmm," replied Nanna Bell. "Lily will never replace your moms, so you don't have to

call her Mom, but you can if you want to. You could also call her Ma Lily, Mimi, or another title. You don't even have to address her in the same manner; you can each address her in your own way."

Nanna Bell watched the children's faces as they considered her words.

"You can also wait and decide later or change your mind after a while too. It's really about what you are comfortable with. I know Lily will be happy with whatever you choose."

"She really will be like my mother," Timothy finally said. "I don't even remember my mother—she died when I was so little. I'm so excited to have Miss Lily be like my mom. I really want to call her Mom."

Zoey's eyes had become misty. "I remember

my mother, of course. I don't remember much about my father, since he died when I was much younger. I know everyone's different. I had a friend who really, really loved her stepmother and called her Mammette Kim. I want Lily to be just like my mom. Although I miss my mom so much, I think it's neat that I get to have another mom in my life. I'd like to call her Mom too." She paused for a moment. "Do you think Uncle John would mind if I called him Dad, Nanna Bell?"

"I think he would love that," Nanna Bell replied. "You two still have a few days before John and Lily return, so you can think about it more. Now, I'm going to keep you both in suspense a little bit longer about the green-eyed creature while we each do our personal morning Bible study. Is that OK?"

The cousins nodded. They loved Bible study. Timothy had always thought the Bible was important, but he had never read it himself, at least not until Nanna Bell had encouraged him to read and study a few verses each day. He had come to love the teachings of Jesus. Today he underlined the words from John 13: "Love one another; as I have loved you, that ye also love one another."

Timothy's eyes wandered from the page to the bright beams of sunlight pouring through the window onto the floor. *My family is not like all other families,* he thought. *It's now made up of my dad, my stepmother, my cousin, and my cousin's grandmother, but we have so much love between us.*

"Time to learn about the green-eyed creature!" Nanna Bell suddenly called from downstairs.

Timothy found Zoey and Nanna Bell at the kitchen table. Nanna Bell pointed to a chart she had created. "This chart shows the eyeshine of different animals. These animals don't have the same eye color during the day. Eyeshine is the color that is reflected when an animal's eyes are struck by light. It makes the eyes look as though they are glowing."

"Like the green eyes we saw last night!" Zoey offered.

"That's right. Depending on the type of light and how it strikes the eye, the colors can be a little different. I made this chart to show the eyeshine of several animals."

Timothy's eyes ran down the column labeled Green Eyeshine. "Let's see. It was too small to be a sheep. It was too big to be a bullfrog. I don't think it was a cat. Oh! Badgers can have green eyeshine. Was it a badger?"

"It sure was!" Nanna Bell said.

"Banana burrito humongous mosquito!" Zoey exclaimed. "We saw a badger at Badger Hills Farm!"

"I called Mrs. Bastian earlier and she remembered Mr. Roach telling her that a badger had been spotted on the farm many years ago," Nanna Bell continued.

"That's why this place was named Badger Hills Farm," Timothy said. "The first family discovered a den of badgers here." He smiled at Zoey. "Like you wrote about in your story."

66

Zoey grinned, happy that he remembered.

"Now there's another one," Timothy continued, "and it could be anywhere!"

"Don't worry," Nanna Bell assured them. "Badgers are as scared of you as you are of them."

"But are they ever dangerous?" Zoey questioned.

"Only if they feel cornered or threatened," Nanna Bell explained. "Then they can be very fierce. If you see a badger, just steer clear. But badger attacks are very, very rare, so you really don't need to worry."

"It's a good thing you didn't bring Sammy," Zoey said in a small voice, looking at Timothy with wide eyes.

"Yeah," Timothy said quietly. "He could

have made the badger feel threatened." He swallowed hard.

Later that day, after Timothy had finished all of his homeschool work, he gathered up some supplies to begin mapping out Badger Hills Farm. He found Nanna Bell sitting on the front porch swing, sending a text. She looked up as Timothy came through the door.

"Oh good! Just the person I wanted to see," she began. "I was just texting your dad."

"Are they enjoying their honeymoon?" Timothy asked.

"Oh yes, and I'm sure they will tell us all about it when they get back home. I just texted to ask him if I could buy you and Zoey phone watches." Nanna Bell smiled. "After hearing a little about yesterday's adventure, he agreed that it would be a good idea."

She glanced at the paper, clipboard, and colored pencils Timothy carried.

"I thought we might head into the city now to buy them, but it looks like you're busy already."

"Oh, I was just going to start mapping the farm, but that can wait," he responded.

"Wonderful! We'll have time to shop for watches before your art lesson with Mrs. Sanchez. Afterward, I thought we could have an early dinner at Buttercup Bakery with Diego."

"Wahoo!" Timothy cried. "I can't wait to tell him about the badger. I'll go get Zoey!"

Nanna Bell chuckled as Timothy ran off excitedly.

Though Diego lived just a short walk from Badger Hills Farm, the friends hadn't seen each other all week. They were used to spending their days together having picnic lunches while learning about God and nature and anything else they were curious about. But the move had kept Timothy and Zoey very busy. Finally, the three homeschooled friends had a chance to catch up.

CHAPTER 7

TIMOTHY FELT A LITTLE ODD WALKING into the Bedford Apartments building and riding the elevator to Mrs. Sanchez's apartment. He had lived in an apartment there most of his life, and it was strange that he no longer called the familiar building home. He knocked on Mrs. Sanchez's door, remembering how he and Zoey had befriended her last spring. He was so thankful to know her; she was a wonderful art teacher, and he always looked forward to their lessons together.

Mrs. Sanchez opened the door with a broad smile. "It's so good to see you back in the building! Tell me all about your move and your new home."

Timothy excitedly launched into the details about Badger Hills Farm—the beautiful mourning dove, the lack of city noises, and the deep darkness of night. He described their new house, including their quest for the secret door.

"A secret door?" asked Mrs. Sanchez.

"Yes, but we couldn't find it. I'm starting to wonder if there really is one. I think we would've found it by now. We've looked everywhere."

"Well, you'll have to let me know if you ever do find it!" Mrs. Sanchez said in her beautiful Spanish accent. "Now, let's get your lesson started. I'd love to teach you about painting animals. Is there a particular animal you'd like to paint?"

"An American badger!" Timothy exclaimed.

"Well, now, that's an interesting choice," Mrs. Sanchez remarked.

Timothy told Mrs. Sanchez all about the badger they had seen the night before.

"A badger will be very fun to paint," she said.

For the next hour, Mrs. Sanchez guided Timothy in painting a badger with three babies on his canvas.

"That's quite good, Timothy," she said, looking over his painting.

Timothy smiled. "Thank you, Mrs. Sanchez. You are a great teacher."

After Timothy's lesson, the group said goodbye to Mrs. Sanchez and had a tasty early dinner at Buttercup Bakery with Diego. The friends were so happy to see each other and didn't want the visit to end.

"Nanna Bell," Timothy asked, "can Diego come back to Badger Hills Farm with us?"

"Certainly! I'll just call his mother to ask her permission."

Back at the farm, Timothy led Diego to the backyard while Zoey went inside to fold her laundry and read.

"Let's play with Sammy!" Timothy said.

As the two boys walked over to Sammy's pen, they could see that the door was pushed wide open, and Sammy was nowhere in sight.

Timothy frowned. "Sammy! Sammy!" he called.

"Where could he have gone?" Diego asked.

"I have no idea." Timothy sighed. "I love that dog so much, but he doesn't obey when I call him, and he runs off far too often. Come on. Let's go find him."

The boys started off on a little trail from the backyard into the woods. It seemed like the best place to start their search.

"You know," Diego began, "my dog had to go to a dog obedience school. Maybe Sammy should go to one."

"That's actually a great idea. I'll have to ask my dad about that when he gets back."

The two friends walked along a small trail for

a while, chatting about the wedding, the move, and the adventure that had led to finding the badger.

"Do you know where we are going?" Diego asked.

Timothy looked around. "Well, not really. I haven't explored much of Badger Hills Farm beyond the gravel road to Mrs. Bastian's house. Zoey and I found the deer fence when we got lost in the pine forest, but that's about it."

The trail slowly disappeared into overgrown weeds, and the boys found themselves surrounded by the forest. They listened as the wind gently whispered through the tall pines.

"Look," Diego said quietly, "it's a California scrub-jay." He pointed to a bird with a gray belly and a bright blue and gray head. "My mom and I have been studying about birds native to this area in our science unit."

"That's cool!" replied Timothy, grateful to have a friend like Diego.

As they came out of the woods, Timothy spotted Sammy running down a hill that led to a small clearing, but there was no time to be excited about finding the little dog. A huge hawk was circling the clearing.

"Oh no!" Timothy yelled as the hawk shot down toward Sammy.

The two boys ran toward the dog, yelling and waving their arms wildly. "Hey! Shoo!"

Sammy, completely unaware of the danger, came bounding toward them, his tongue hanging out the side of his mouth.

The hawk tucked its wings in closer to its

body and dove faster toward the puppy.

"Noooo!" Timothy ran faster, yelling as loud as he could. Suddenly, the majestic bird veered away and flew back up into the sky.

Timothy collapsed on the ground as Sammy reached him. He scooped the puppy up into his arms and breathed a sigh of relief.

Diego plopped on the ground beside him. "Whew! That was close!"

Sammy leaped over to Diego's lap, jumping up to lick his face.

Timothy stood up and scooped Sammy into his arms again. "You have no idea how close you were to serious danger, little fella." He hugged Sammy close, and the puppy snuggled up against him.

"He's been having the time of his life

running through the trees, chasing squirrels, and barking at birds," Diego chuckled.

"Probably," Timothy replied. "I'm glad we found him when we did."

Diego nodded. "Me too!" He looked around, noticing that the sun was sinking low in the sky. "We better head back before it gets dark."

Later that night, after Diego had left, Timothy and Zoey helped Nanna Bell start a fire in the big brick fireplace.

Nanna Bell read the next chapter of the Christmas book as the cousins listened from the big, snuggly chairs near the fire. It was an exciting adventure about a boy who lived on a reindeer farm in Norway. At the end of the chapter, the boy's family enjoyed their traditional Christmas dish of cold rice pudding with whipped cream and red berry sauce.

"Mmmm, that sounds delicious!" Zoey remarked.

"I'm glad you think so," Nanna Bell replied, closing the book and tucking it back into their reading basket, "because I made some of that very pudding for us to enjoy tomorrow."

"You are the best, Nanna Bell," said Zoey.

"Well, I'm doing my very best to make your Christmas season special. I'm just sorry we don't have a Christmas tree."

"Wait!" blurted Timothy. "There are so many pine trees here on the farm. I bet we could find a little tree somewhere that would make a perfect Christmas tree!"

"That's a great idea!" Zoey exclaimed.

"Can we look for one tomorrow?" Timothy asked.

"I don't see why not," Nanna Bell replied. "But whenever you go off exploring, I want you to have your phone watches with you and make sure you keep them charged. Even with the watch, I never want you wandering out alone."

"Because we might get attacked by that badger?" Timothy asked, half jokingly.

"No." Nanna Bell laughed. "But you could get hurt or come across a venomous snake."

"I promise," the children said in unison.

Nanna Bell chuckled again. "Good, now off to bed with you both. I'll be in soon to say good night."

Timothy hurried into his flannel pajamas

and climbed into bed. He looked around the room as he waited for Nanna Bell to come upstairs. Even in the dim light, he could see the shadows on the wall and ceiling. They still looked just as scary.

A sudden knock at the door startled him. "Come in," he said after a moment.

Nanna Bell poked her head around the open door and smiled. "All ready for bed?"

Timothy nodded in response. "Nanna Bell, could you turn on the bathroom light and leave the door cracked a little?"

"Sure, Timothy," she said as she turned on the light. "Is everything all right?"

Timothy felt he could share anything with Nanna Bell. "I don't know why, but I've been afraid of the dark since we moved here."

84

"That's understandable," Nanna Bell assured him. "This is a new place with new things."

"But will I ever be able to sleep without the bathroom light on?" Timothy asked.

"I think so," she responded, giving Timothy a hug. "You might just need some time."

"Thank you, Nanna Bell. That makes me feel better."

"You're welcome," she replied. "Sleep well."

As Nanna Bell left, closing the door behind her, Timothy realized that he had forgotten to say his prayers. He knelt beside his bed and talked to God about his fear of the dark.

Back in bed, Timothy didn't feel any less scared.

Suddenly, he had an idea. *What if I close the bathroom door a little more each night as I get used to it here at my new home?*

Nanna Bell had left the door halfway open, so he got up and closed it a few more inches.

Once he was snugly back in bed, Timothy looked out at the moonlight pouring over the tips of the pine trees. *I do love watching the pine boughs sway in the wind*, he thought. Then another thought came into his mind. *I think God gave me the idea to shut the bathroom door a little more each night. He's always there for me.*

CHAPTER 8

NANNA BELL WENT TO HER BOOK CLUB in the city early the next day. Timothy and Zoey started out to look for a Christmas tree. Unfortunately, they had to leave Sammy at home, as he was too likely to run off and not come back when called.

Whistling merrily, Zoey carried a small picnic basket that Nanna Bell had kindly packed that morning.

Timothy carried a clipboard with blank white

paper and a mechanical pencil so he could start creating sketches for his map.

Instead of taking the gravel road toward Mrs. Bastian's house and the front gate, the two decided to explore a smaller dirt road behind their house that led deeper into the farm. They hadn't gone far when Zoey spoke up.

"Look, it's all overgrown with grass." She pointed ahead to where the rutted dirt road disappeared into a thick tangle of grass. "Now where do we go?"

Timothy looked around. His eyes rested on an old, crumbling stone wall that stretched into a pine forest. "Let's go that way," he replied, motioning toward the stone wall. "I can sketch the wall as we go."

"I was thinking we should head over to that

other pine forest," Zoey suggested, pointing to a forest of pine trees in the other direction.

Timothy didn't think that was a great idea. "It's farther away," he said.

"Yeah, but it looks so pretty over there, and those are the kinds of trees that have huge pine cones. I want to go that way."

"If we find a Christmas tree over there, we'll have to drag it so much farther," Timothy argued. "And I want to sketch the stone wall."

"You go that way, then," Zoey said as she started walking away. "I'll go gather some pine cones and then find you by the stone wall."

"We're supposed to stay together, though," Timothy called, thinking that Zoey wasn't being very nice.

Zoey didn't even look back as she called,

"Don't worry. I'll stay where I can see the stone wall. I'll catch up with you later."

A frustrated sigh escaped Timothy's lips as he watched Zoey skipping through the field of golden grass. *I should probably go with her, but it's not fair that she's just going off the way she wants to go. She'll just have to find me when she's done,* Timothy thought. He turned and started walking toward the stone wall.

As the sun rose higher in the sky, Timothy walked slowly along the wall, carefully sketching on his clipboard. Every few minutes, he looked for Zoey and saw her nearing the distant pine forest.

Eventually, the stone wall led to a little stream that ran along the edge of the small pine tree forest where he hoped to find a

Christmas tree. And then he saw it. Right there, a few steps into the forest, the sun shone brightly on a beautiful fir tree. *It's perfect!* Timothy thought. *It's small, but that's great for our first year here.*

Excitedly, Timothy looked over his shoulder to see if Zoey was coming, but he didn't see her anywhere.

I'll wait right here, Timothy thought. *I can't wait to show her this perfect Christmas tree.*

After an hour of waiting, Timothy was hungry and trying very hard not to get upset. He groaned as he realized that Zoey had taken the picnic basket with her.

A grassy bank by the stream beckoned to him, and he lay down with his arms behind his head. Beams of late morning sunlight

filtered through the puffy clouds and wrapped Timothy in warmth. Birds twittered, and the water nearby trickled peacefully.

Before long, Timothy drifted off to sleep.

Suddenly, he sat bolt upright, realizing he had dozed off and wondering how much time had passed. Standing up, he looked around but didn't see Zoey anywhere.

Our watches! he thought. Five times he dialed Zoey's number, but she didn't answer.

Trying not to panic, Timothy prayed in his heart, *What should I do now? Should I go try to find her?*

Once again, he remembered his watch. *I'll call Nanna Bell!*

"Don't panic," she said. "I'm on my way home from the book club already. I'll call

Diego and his father since they live so close by. They can help us look for Zoey. Hurry on home, and then we can all go back out together."

Timothy alternated between running and jogging in his hurry to get home. To his surprise, the back door was open, but Nanna Bell wasn't home. *I must've forgotten to shut the door when we left this morning*, thought Timothy as he walked into the kitchen. He hadn't eaten since breakfast, and he was starving. *I'll grab something to eat while I wait for Nanna Bell*, he thought as he reached for the fridge handle. *Then I'll let Sammy out.* Suddenly, a growling, hissing sound filled the room. At the same time, loud barks and yips filled the yard from Sammy's pen.

Timothy whipped around with lightning speed and saw a badger huddled over a bowl of fruit on the table.

Timothy's mind swirled with panic. He remembered the open back door and what

Nanna Bell had said about badgers—they could be dangerous when they felt cornered. This badger, with its bared teeth and growling noises, certainly seemed like it felt cornered.

In a flash, Timothy ran into the kitchen pantry, slammed the door behind him, and then ran to the back of the pantry. He breathed a sigh of relief as he leaned against the brick wall.

Suddenly, the wall shifted behind him!

Timothy scrambled forward as he lost his balance. He turned to stare at what should have been a solid brick wall. Instead, he saw that a rectangle of bricks was pushed a few inches into the wall. He lightly pushed that section of the wall again, and it began to move backward.

"Banana burrito humongous mosquito!" cried Timothy, borrowing the phrase of

wonder that he had learned from Zoey. "This must be the secret door!"

Timothy peeked around the section of the wall that had opened and gasped in surprise. There was a tiny room that had nothing in it except a door—a big, solid wooden door with golden hinges and a golden handle. The room was very dim, but Timothy could still see a layer of dust on the floor and on the golden door handle.

"Timothy!" Nanna Bell's comforting voice came from the kitchen. "Timothy, are you here?"

Bursting out of the pantry door, Timothy found Nanna Bell, Diego, and Diego's dad in the kitchen.

"I left the door open this morning, and

there's a badger in the house!" he cried.

"It's OK," Diego assured his friend. "As we were pulling up to the house, we saw it running across the yard into the forest. It's not in the house anymore."

Timothy wanted so badly to tell everyone about the secret door, but he knew that they needed to find Zoey.

"Let's go find Zoey," said Nanna Bell as she pushed a blanket and some flashlights into a backpack. "I hope we won't need these flashlights, but let's go!"

Timothy led the group to the end of the dirt road and explained what had happened.

"I'll stay here and keep a lookout," stated Nanna Bell. "Why don't you three go to the forest where Zoey went?"

With a prayer in their minds the whole time, Timothy and Diego followed Diego's father across the field of long golden grass. Timothy shivered as they entered the pine forest. The trees were thick and blocked out much of the sunlight.

"Which way?" Diego's father wondered aloud.

"Look! It's our picnic basket!" Timothy cried as he pointed at the ground near a stream so wide Timothy thought it was more river than stream.

Suddenly, Zoey's voice cut through the forest. "I'm over here!"

And there she was, sitting on the other side of the stream, holding her ankle in obvious pain.

102

A fallen log made a bridge across the wide stream and led to where Zoey was. As the group started crossing the log, she called out to them.

"Careful! The log is slippery. I fell into the water and twisted my ankle badly. I can't walk on it."

After giving Zoey a hug, Timothy asked, "Why didn't you answer your phone watch?"

"I smashed it on a rock when I fell in the water," Zoey explained. "I'm so sorry we didn't stay together like Nanna Bell asked," she added meekly.

Timothy had been frustrated earlier, but now he felt sorry for Zoey. She was shivering in her wet clothes and was obviously in a lot of pain.

"We're so glad you are OK, Zoey," Diego's

dad said. "Now, we've got to get you back home. Nanna Bell is waiting for us back at the dirt road with a nice warm blanket."

Timothy smiled as he thought about the secret door. *I'll wait until Zoey is taken care of before I tell her about the secret door.*

CHAPTER 9

TIMOTHY KNELT BESIDE HIS BED. NANNA Bell had taught him a lot about prayer, so he didn't rush through his prayers like he used to. Tonight, he thought about the events of that day. He remembered praying for help to know what to do when Zoey didn't answer her phone watch, and he realized that the idea to call Nanna Bell had been an answer to his prayers. He thanked God for His help and asked again for His help with overcoming his fear of the dark. Then Timothy got up and switched the bathroom light on, shutting the door a little more than he had the night before. Only a narrow beam of light fell into his room now, but he felt calm and safe as he snuggled down into his covers.

Only four more days until Dad and Miss Lily arrive home! he thought happily as he closed his eyes.

The next day, Zoey lay on the couch with her twisted ankle propped up on pillows. Sammy was curled up nearby, chewing on his rope toy. Nanna Bell served breakfast on trays so they could all eat together in the family room.

Timothy sat down with his tray and simply could not hold the news in any longer.

"I found the secret door!"

"What!" Zoey cried. "How? Where? When?"

After Timothy explained how he had found the door, Nanna Bell went to investigate. She came back with a big smile. "Yes, that does look like the secret door. I guess our badger friend really helped us out. What do you guys want to do now?"

"I've already thought about it," Timothy said. "I think we should wait until Zoey's foot is healed enough to walk on. I want her to be able to see what's behind the door at the same time I do."

Zoey smiled at Timothy. "I can't wait to discover what's behind the door. Thank you for waiting, Timothy!"

"You're very thoughtful, Timothy," Nanna

Bell said. "In the meantime, we can keep ourselves busy by getting and decorating that Christmas tree you found."

"How will we get it?" Timothy asked.

"Well, I thought I would go to the city and buy a saw, a rope, and a thick tarp from the hardware store. It might take us a while and be a lot of work, but I bet you and I could cut it down and drag it home."

"I bet we could!" Timothy cried.

"And Sammy and I can string popcorn and make ornaments while you go," Zoey offered. Sammy perked up and let out a little yip after hearing his name.

"Great idea!" Nanna Bell said. "I like our plan!"

Sawing the tree down was more work than

Timothy expected. He was sweating, even though it was cool outside, and he needed many breaks. He liked the work, though, and felt quite proud and satisfied when the tree was tied up in the thick tarp. He and Nanna Bell started pulling it home, stopping every few minutes for a break.

Finally, they were back at the house and ready to bring the tree inside. Before they finished sliding it into the house, Nanna Bell and Timothy went inside to check on Sammy and Zoey. They found Sammy fast asleep next to the couch and Zoey covered in a mound of carefully strung popcorn garland and white paper snowflake ornaments.

"I'm so glad you're back!" she said joyfully. "I can't wait to decorate the tree."

"Me either!" Timothy said. "Let me just put Sammy in his pen, and then we can finish bringing the tree in." He woke Sammy gently and led him away to his pen.

Nanna Bell eyed the pile of snowy-white garland and ornaments. "You did a wonderful job, Zoey. The tree is going to look beautiful.

Timothy and I will be right back, and then we can get started setting up and decorating."

Getting the tree inside wasn't nearly as hard as getting it home. In no time at all, they had it set up and decorated with the beautiful white paper snowflakes and popcorn garland Zoey had made. Nanna Bell even surprised them with strings of little white lights she had bought at the hardware store.

Blessedly, Zoey's ankle had not been twisted too badly. Within a few days, she was walking on it again.

Finally, they were ready to explore the secret door.

"Dad and Miss Lily get home tomorrow night," Timothy said to Nanna Bell, not quite ready to call Miss Lily "Mom" when speaking

of her. "Do you think we need to wait until they get here?"

With a shake of her head, Nanna Bell replied, "No, you two go ahead." She handed a lantern to each of them. "I'll watch through the door while you go in. I want you to be the explorers."

Zoey had to tug on the golden handle a little, but then the door swung open. All was dark within, so the children lit their lanterns. The light illuminated stone stairs leading down to a short hallway or tunnel of some sort.

"This is so exciting," Timothy whispered, not sure why he was whispering.

"I don't like the spiderwebs, though," Zoey whispered back. "It doesn't look like anyone has been in here for quite a while. Look, I see

the end of the tunnel!"

"It's another door!" Timothy exclaimed.

This door was metal and quite rusty.

When Zoey tried the door handle, it wouldn't turn. Timothy pushed and pulled on the door, but it didn't move or shift at all. Nothing they tried would budge the door.

"I guess we'll need to wait for Dad," Timothy said with a sigh. "He'll be able to get it open. Let's go tell Nanna Bell what we found."

CHAPTER 10

"THEY'RE HERE! THEY'RE HERE!"
Timothy cried as he turned from the window.

Timothy flew out the door. Zoey followed along a little more slowly, limping slightly. Sammy barked and wagged his tail as he ran in excited circles around their legs. Nanna Bell trailed along behind the cousins, a welcoming smile spread across her face.

John and Lily caught the children up in huge

hugs. Fiery pink and orange streaks of light from the setting sun seemed to be celebrating the happy reunion.

Everyone started talking at once, and they all laughed.

"You first," John said to Zoey. "I thought

I saw you limping a little as you came out to greet us. Is everything all right?"

"Let's talk over a late dinner," Nanna Bell suggested. "I've made some Irish stew and rolls, if anyone's interested."

"Wow, how can I say no to that!" John declared with a big grin.

The twinkling stars appeared in the night sky one by one as stories flew around the dinner table: Zoey's adventure in the forest and her apologies again for not following Nanna Bell's rules, Sammy's getting under the deer fence and seeing the badger come out when they had to go close the gate in the middle of the night, Sammy's nearly getting caught by a hawk, and, of course, all about cutting and decorating the Christmas tree.

There was more too. Timothy talked about learning to chop wood and how Sammy was always running off and not obeying. Zoey and Nanna Bell both had stories to add. Then everyone realized they hadn't heard anything about John and Lily's honeymoon yet.

"Come see the Christmas tree!" Nanna Bell suggested. "We can hear all about your honeymoon while we enjoy the warm fire and glow of the tree."

After admiring the Christmas tree, John and Lily took some wrapped gifts out of their suitcases and placed them under the tree.

"We did a little Christmas shopping on our honeymoon," Lily explained with a smile.

"Tell us all about your trip!" Zoey cried.

It was quite late when the stories were over.

Timothy had been waiting to tell his father and Lily about the secret door. Nanna Bell and Zoey had agreed to let Timothy tell them, since he was the one who found the door first. But Timothy wanted to wait until the morning, when everything was bright. Plus, he was tired.

After Timothy said his prayers, he got three separate tuck-ins: one from Nanna Bell, one from his father, and one from Lily.

Lily came in last and sat on the chair beside his bed. They laughed and talked for a couple of minutes, and then Lily smoothed Timothy's hair with her cool hand and kissed him lightly on the forehead as she stood up.

"I'm so grateful to be a part of your family, Timothy," she said gently. "I can never replace your mother, but I want to love you just as a mother would and help you in every way I can."

"Zoey and I have been talking," Timothy said in reply. "We were wondering if . . . well, would it be OK if we called you Mom?"

Lily reached for Timothy's hand and squeezed it gently. "Absolutely!"

After Lily left, Timothy started to get out of bed to turn on the bathroom light, but then he stopped and got back in bed. *I don't think I need the light anymore.*

The shadows of tree branches swaying on his wall didn't seem scary anymore—they seemed peaceful.

Timothy gazed out at the few twinkling stars he could see above the pine trees. Soon his eyes fluttered closed as he fell asleep, dreaming of the huge rusty metal door: telling his parents about it, the possibilities of what might lie beyond it, and the adventures they would embark on next.

Continue the adventures of Timothy and Zoey
with *The Hidden Room*—Book 2 of the Badger
Hills Farm series by Jenny Phillips.

Available at
goodandbeautiful.com